Jenny

Jenny

Harry "Buddy" Beckett

Artistic Spaces Publishing
Murfreesboro, TN

Cover and interior illustrations by Elizabeth "Betty" Ann Thompson (Adapted for print with permission)

Book Design: Artistic Spaces Publishing

Notice: This is a work of fiction. Names, characters, places, and incidents are either products of the author's imagination or, if real, are used fictitiously.

ISBN 10: 0-9796328-2-x
ISBN 13: 978-0-9796328-2-2

Library of Congress Control Number: 2007907048

Subject Headings
     1. Historical Fiction
     2. Romance

Published by: Artistic Spaces Publishing Company
               P.O. Box 330703
               Murfreesboro, TN 37133-0703

Printed in the United States of America

This book is dedicated to Catherine Eileen Petrany who inspires me to seek loftier goals.

Contents

Chapter 1

. . . eerie quietness enveloped them

Dark clouds, driven by a sudden wind, tumbled across the late afternoon sky. Six Conestoga wagons stopped near a rocky cliff where small, twisted trees and bushes were growing on narrow ledges. A man and a young girl immediately started walking the short distance toward the cliff. Each had a short length of rope to be used to carry firewood back to the wagons.

A few seconds after the two walked through an opening (or draw) in the cliff, the girl screamed, "HELP! HELP! SOME-ONE HELP US!"

At that instant, a man on horseback near the wagons turned his horse toward the screams. In response to the urging of spurs, the sorrel flew toward the distress plea and was quickly out of sight of the wagons. Before anyone else in the wagon train could respond to the call for help, a yelling band of Indians suddenly charged toward the wagons. There were enough of them to continuously ride on both sides of the straight-line wagon train. Even if there had been more time before the attack, six wagons could not be positioned into a night circle for protection against the Indians.

In less than ten minutes, all wagon train members were dead or dying, and all the wagons were burning. This violent slaughter occurred around 6:00 p.m., the second day of June 1883.

Twenty-eight days earlier, the six wagons had left Independence, Missouri on the way to Montana and California. The wagons, which included twenty-six men, women, and children, were on the well-traveled Oregon Trail. After three weeks of mostly dry weather, a little over 300 miles had been covered when they crossed the Platte River near Grand Island, Nebraska. Their goal was to stay on the Oregon Trail for seven weeks to Fort Laramie, Wyoming Territory, which was about 670 miles from Independence. Until a few minutes ago, the trip had been pleasant and uneventful.

The hundreds of thousands who had traveled the trail since the 1840s always had trouble gathering wood for cooking fires. Dried buffalo dung (buffalo chips) was a suitable substitute, but after forty years of senseless buffalo killing, it was now more scarce than wood. When the man and girl spotted some wood on the rocky ledges, they hurried to gather some much needed fuel for supper fires. When earlier immigrants and pioneers stretched across the Oregon Trail, they were just passing through Indian lands and were seldom attacked. Since Kansas became a state in 1861 and Nebraska in 1867, more and more people were settling in the new states and threatened the Indian's way of life.

The group of six wagons attacked by Indians had just crossed the Platte River over a bridge. Before the bridge was built, crossing the mile-wide shallow Platte with quicksand banks and muck bottom was one of the most hazardous obstacles on the trail for the earlier travelers. But Indians did not attack thousands and thousands of wagons that pulled and pushed through the mile of muck.

By 1883, the transcontinental railroad carried most immigrants and others to the promising West where land was free or cheap. But train fares were too expensive for some families, especially those who traveled with milk cows and extra horses. Also, the strong oxen that pulled the prairie schooners would later be used to till virgin soil.

When the young girl jumped from her wagon to gather firewood, she didn't know the thrill and excitement of her westward trip was going to soon be replaced with grief and sadness. All of her tomorrows would also depend on a brave decision she would soon have to make.

The rider who sprinted to the call for help had only joined the wagon train two days earlier. He left Marietta, Ohio a year ago and had been drifting between St. Louis and Independence, Missouri until uniting with the wagon train. Jeremiah "Jerry" Bowles was a handsome young man. His clear, blue eyes and black, wavy hair would always cause females to linger an extra second when they looked at him—some would stare. White, even teeth were revealed often by his quick smile and were in notable contrast to his sun-tanned face. Jerry's six-foot frame was straight and trim, from his broad shoulders to his narrow hips. He was not a cowboy or a pioneer, but a drifter with a couple of talents—sketching and making music. Next to his rifle, blanket and canteen, he always had his artist tools and fiddle on his horse. His harmonica was holstered in his vest pocket. By a narrow margin, the wagon train leaders agreed he could join them in exchange for portrait settings.

When Jerry found the unconscious young girl and man up the draw, he almost fell off his horse from the horror that filled his eyes. The girl was lying on the rocky ground. He didn't know if she was unconscious or dead. The man was on his back with one leg between two large rocks. He looked more dead than alive, and Jerry knew he would surely die soon. He had multiple rattlesnake bites around his arms and neck. One large rattler was still entwined around his chest and arm. Jerry was ready to shoot another rattler beside the groaning man when he heard the attacking Indians. He wisely changed his mind and didn't alert the Indians to his concealed location.

The dying groans from the snakebite victim were not loud, because the swelling in his neck was constricting his breathing. They would not be heard at all in a few more minutes. His neck and face were already swollen twice the normal size. Jerry didn't know what to do. The man would soon be gone, and the girl was probably already dead.

He could hear the battle around the wagons and wondered if he should try to help. He couldn't see, but it sounded like there were a large number of Indians. He was also hearing fewer rifle and pistol shots.

Before he could decide what to do next, torrential rain and high winds prompted him to dismount. The girl was lying on her side. Her rain-soaked, blue checkered gingham dress was clinging to her small body. He covered her with his blanket. Seemingly in a trance, Jerry Bowles, a drifter who had seen and experienced quite a bit of trauma in his twenty-two years, stood like a statue looking at his blanket.

The resounding noise of gunshots and wild, whooping screams diminished until there were only the lonesome sounds of wailing wind and the spatter of rain. Jerry's eyes momentarily became bleary, and objects were out of focus. His head started to spin. The scene of horror surrounding him was so unexpected and so unreal that his whole body suddenly seemed to be swirling downward into a cold darkness. A loud clap of thunder reconnected Jerry with the present.

The unfortunate man still had a rattlesnake on his chest, but he had stopped groaning. The man's face was so grotesque Jerry could not hold back his tears.

While still standing beside the girl, he remembered she wasn't swollen when he covered her with his blanket. He quickly reasoned snakes might not have bitten her. He checked his tears and kneeled beside her and gently removed the blanket from her face. To his surprise, big brown eyes were quizzically looking at him. He immediately began to gather her in his arms, when she screamed.

"STAY AWAY! DON'T TOUCH ME! WHAT HAPPEN TO DUKE?"

Jerry backed away and didn't answer her question. It was still raining and getting darker and cooler. From a stirring in his compassionate heart, he felt an immense responsibility to this frightened girl. She had apparently fainted after witnessing the initial snakebites and Duke's desperate and futile defense against overwhelming odds. After her outburst, she seemed disoriented and was shaking. He then noticed bloodstained hair above her right ear. Jerry couldn't know for sure, but it didn't look life threatening. He believed her larger problem was from shock. After asking about Duke, she cowered and closed her eyes.

Jerry tried to corral his various thoughts and focus on some solution to the predicament surrounding him. He had been with the girl and Duke maybe ten minutes, but it seemed like hours. He felt a first priority to the girl but was concerned about possible injured survivors at the wagons. He had to have a plan soon; in less than an hour it would be totally dark. A shelter and a fire were needed quickly, because the girl was shivering again.

The rain and wind subsided, and eerie quietness enveloped them. Jerry stood close to the girl, fearing more rattlesnakes were ready to come from the rock crevices. Daylight was fading fast, and long shadows were creeping across the craggy rocks. Jerry looked at the girl's glazed eyes—she seemed to be searching for some reference of understanding or stability.

The place was getting spookier by the minute, as his eyes scanned the rocks for more snakes. He couldn't look at Duke again. Jerry did look at the little scared girl with compassion and knew she had to be moved to a dry place. He could think of two good reasons for not going to the wagons for shelter. First, his tracks in the rain soaked ground would be an invitation to be captured by Indians. Second, the wagons were probably burned.

With no more hesitation, he stiffened his resolve and knelt beside the girl. He knew she didn't know about the Indians because she had already fainted when he arrived.

"Missy, can you hear me? Missy, we need to go to the wagons to get you warm. Can you hear me Missy? Let me take you to your family and get you dry by a warm fire."

The frightened girl apparently comprehended the part about a warm fire and offered no resistance when Jerry scooped her up into his strong arms. He placed her on the saddle and mounted behind her. When outside the draw, he guided the horse close to the rocky cliff in the direction he had just traveled. He didn't know what was ahead but knew a suitable shelter was back down the trail about half a mile. It was a rather large cave situated a short distance off the wagon trail. He was sure the Indians were aware of it, but a calculated risk had to be taken.

A kind soul, of hopefully a more joyous camping experience, had left some dry wood. In a short time, Jerry had a large fire blazing in the night. It was much brighter than he would normally allow in hostile territory, but they needed quick heat to dry their clothes and blanket. The girl sat near the fire and didn't talk as she stared at him. He shared some hard tack and beef jerky with her.

When Jerry opened his eyes after a nearly sleepless night, bright sunlight was a welcome sight. He asked his little ward,

"Missy, tell me your name. My name is Jeremiah Bowles. I'm originally from Marietta, Ohio, and everybody calls me Jerry. I was part of the wagon train but only for the past two days."

Jerry waited for a reply that didn't come. "I will not harm you. I'm going to help you all I can. Tell me your name so I won't keep calling you Missy."

Still no response—but he kept talking and hoping a subliminal level of awareness would surface and connect her to the present. She still seemed frightened and apparently unsure how much trust she could extend to a stranger. They needed food and a lot of distance from this place. It didn't matter to him which direction to go.

He knew four of the six wagons were headed for Montana, and two were bound for California. But he didn't know where his mute ward was going. She had to talk and make the decision to continue onward or return back east. If she never talked again, he knew what should be done next, and he became so nauseated he briefly considered returning to Independence without concern for Missy's welfare. With a charred stick, he wrote a message on a large rock that he was returning to the wagons and would be back soon. If she regained full consciousness while he was gone, she would know he had not abandoned her.

Jerry was gone for only two hours. The wagon scene was actually worse than he had anticipated. He counted twenty-four dead men, women, and children. At least one man or grown boy was at each wagon. At the fourth wagon, only a teenage boy and a young lady lay deadlocked in each other's arms. Jerry stirred the partially burned remains with a stick and found a singed family portrait. He then retrieved thirty-one, twenty-dollar gold coins and sixty-seven silver dollars from the pockets of the dead men. He next gathered several pounds of food staples. All food, skillets, pots, and a coffeepot were placed in boxes and wired to the axle of two front wagon wheels. With the tongue of the front axle strapped to his saddle, he returned to the cave.

Missy walked into the cave as Jerry put down the last box of food. He spoke, but she didn't answer. She appeared to be physically all right—just not talking. She had removed the blood from her hair, which was now tied back. Jerry went to the back of the cave and settled down to sleep. He knew his undetected visit to the wagons was luck. His plan was to sleep now and return to bury the dead after dark. Although the girl wasn't talking, he sensed she was starting to trust him more.

Jerry Bowles, as a drifter, had seen and done some things that would turn the stomach of most people. But burying twenty-four bloated corpses at night was like nothing he had ever imagined. The contorted expressions illuminated by the faint light of night were a ghostly horror he would never forget. But the remains of Duke were worse than the dead people at the wagons. The buzzards had pecked and eaten a great deal of him, including his eyes. Jerry shut his own eyes and threw rocks on the black, swollen body until it was completely covered. All twenty-five graves were unmarked.

Jerry had never been so drained in his twenty-two years. He had just completed the hardest ten hours of his life. If the ground had not been soft, he guessed he would still be digging. His endurance and emotions had been stretched to dangerous limits. He had even had some crying sessions. He was tired and dirty and was stressed over the uncertainty that awaited him at the cave.

Chapter 2

". . . you will just have to trust me . . . "

It was almost dawn when Jerry tied Topsi to a tree outside the cave. Apprehensively, he slowly walked inside. In the dim light of a new day, he could see the food items had been moved and stacked in short rows. He didn't see Missy. But a few minutes later, as he laid his tired body down, the little girl entered the cave.

During the night, she had recovered from seeing her brother dying, only to realize her other family members were probably also dead. Jerry had placed the family portrait where she could find it, and she later said she recognized some food from her wagon. She connected some facts with some assumptions, and the revelation was so painful, she had cried during most of the night. She didn't know any details of what had happened with the wagons and didn't even remember how she got to the cave.

Jerry was going to talk to her again, but was so tired he almost immediately drifted into a deep sleep. The sizzle and smell of frying bacon woke him two hours later. To his surprise, he also heard some soft words.

"Do you like sowbelly and slam-johns?"

He couldn't answer for a few breaths. Her voice was sweet with only a slight twang. Still shocked, but appreciative she was talking, he boldly answered her question.

"Yes! I sure do like bacon and flapjacks."

She didn't look up from the cooking fire and didn't say anymore. Jerry just looked at her and listened to the frying bacon. She brought him a cup of coffee. They started their first breakfast together in silence until Jerry complimented her on the excellent slam-johns. He offered to clean up, but she shook her head indicating no help was needed.

After a while, the little cook sat on a rock, twenty feet from Jerry, with a tin cup of coffee. (She was told, before starting her westward trip, to learn to like coffee and tea because water was often too foul-tasting to drink without some flavor.) To his surprise, she looked straight at him and asked, "I need to know two things Mister. What happened, and what are your intentions?"

Her voice didn't quiver as she pointedly asked her question. Jerry detected a determined and more matured young girl than the wet, gingham-clad one he had carried to the cave. He was ready to answer when she more boldly repeated her question.

"Mister! What happened to my family, and what do you plan to do next?"

"Okay Missy, I'm going to tell you. I hope you are strong enough to hear the truth."

After all her grim assumptions last night, she was ready for the truth. Through tight lips, she firmly replied, "Yes I am, go on."

"First, my name is Jeremiah Bowles and I'm originally from Marietta, Ohio. I go by Jerry. Two, no, three days ago, I hooked up with the wagons. I am neither a homesteader nor a cowboy—I'm just driftin' my way out farther west."

He momentarily stopped for any more questions. She had maintained eye contact during his few words and was showing no signs of change.

"Okay, I was close to half a mile behind the wagons when they stopped. I hurriedly caught up and heard your cry for help."

Jerry stopped again—still no reaction, so he continued. "When I got to you and the man, he was almost gone and you . . . you had fainted. You were lying on the rocky ground. Do you remember about the snakes?"

She lowered her head and answered, just above a whisper. "Yes." She then quickly looked at Jerry. "We had not picked up one piece of firewood when a rattler got Duke on his leg. He bent over and another one got his arm. He dropped to his knees, and two more were on his neck and shoulders. It was so awful . . . That's when I . . ."

"I know Missy. There was nothing I could do. I started to shoot one when I heard the Indians."

She had been staring at the ground until she heard "Indians." Jerry hesitated while she readied herself for the unhappy news about her family.

Before he continued, she blurted, "Duke was my older brother. He was only twenty-one."

"I'm sorry. I wish I could have saved him."

She turned and looked outside the cave momentarily, before resuming eye contact with the man who was going to tell what happened to her family members on the wagon train.

Jerry Bowles was a drifter, who happened to be at the right place at the right time to save this young girl's life. He told her the Indians had taken the lives of all twenty-four settlers on the wagons.

"The men and women fought bravely. The Indians took their dead with them when they left, but I saw evidence where at least twelve Indians had died near the wagons. I guess 'bout three dozen or more Indians were in the attacking party."

Jenny listened intently. She knew her brother and sister had fought bravely for their lives. With her eyes closed, she heard Jerry reverently say, "Each of the twenty-four brave defenders was properly buried, and at the end, I said a prayer for all the surviving family members. I prayed for each survivor to find the strength to carry on and to do God's will until all can meet again in Heav—"

She interrupted. "I'll tell you, Mister, right now I'm not too happy about God's will. I lost two brothers and a sister, and I don't understand why God willed that on me."

"Missy, Missy, wait a minute! What about God's will that I came and found you, and I'm pledging my help to you? You could have died from those rattlesnakes or wandered back to the wagons, and the Indians would have got you. What about that, Missy?"

The little girl, who had just declared her attitude concerning the events that had left her stranded on the Oregon Trail, lowered her head and mumbled, "I'm sorry. I'm trying to understand, and I am grateful for your help, and . . . "

During her lull he interrupted, "What's your name?"

"Jenny—Jenny Supples. I lost my brothers Duke and Fielding and sister Ida. My older brother Charles is in Montana. He left home when he was sixteen. I was only five when he left. A circus came to the next county and he left with it. He's now 'stablished in Montana and sent for us. My oldest brother, Herbert, is married and living next to Mommy and Poppy in Winfield, West Virginia."

Jenny was relaxing some, and a slight glow of contentment seemed to burnish her cheeks with a little color when mentioning her parents. Jerry was thinking a bit of her fear was gone as she told about her family—and she wasn't finished.

"Albert and Robert are married, living in Kanawha County near where the circus came. Mary and Eve are married and live in Cabell County. Me and Nellie are not married. Nellie is eleven."

"Wow! That's a big family—ten or eleven."

"Eleven and now eight. Tell me Mister, why did this happen? We weren't bothering the Indians."

Well Judy, we were trespassing on their native land, and they thought we were going to stop and take another thousand acres from them. Immigrants have been settling here in Nebraska since it became a state in 1867."

She looked at him with her head slightly lowered and pertly replied, "My name is Jenny—Jenny Supples."

"I'm sorry Jenny, my name is Jerry—not Mister. It's Jerry Bowles."

For the first time since Jerry met this pretty little gal, she smiled—just a quick smile in acknowledging that she now knew his name. When he first saw her, he noticed her beautiful eyes that now beamed with a luster. With this enhancement of her facial features, she was gorgeous.

Jerry realized he was staring when he quickly jerked his head and exclaimed, "Listen Jenny, we could talk all day about why the Indians attacked, but we have to leave this place and soon. You have to make a very important decision about what to do next. I will help any which way you decide. I'm just driftin' with the wind and help you get back to West Virginia or can help you continue westward. I'll go either direction."

Jenny Supples, the tenth child of Robert and Manerva Jane Bonham Supples, had always loved the great outdoors. She played with bugs more than with dolls. She could recognize the trill of all the birds living near her home in Winfield, West Virginia. She knew their feeding and nesting habits from many enjoyable hours roaming fields and woods. Her brothers Duke and Fielding would often let her tag along and taught her a lot about trees, berries, flowers, and wildlife. Just last year, at twelve years old, she shot her first rabbit.

Her older brother Charles left home when she was five, and she didn't know much about him except from his letters.

He would write one or two times a year telling about his travels and adventures. He stayed with the circus for three years, becoming a clown and a trapeze performer. After that flying chapter in his life, he started moving toward the great Wild West. Last year, Jenny's dad received three letters from Charles urging him to relocate the family to Montana Territory. He had started a butcher shop in the new town of Billings and was expanding his business to include a general store. Billings was founded in 1882 by the Northern Pacific Railway and was growing fast. He said in the second and third letters that there was still "lots of good land left."

Jenny's parents had no desire to move from their comfortable homestead with better than good farmland. Not so with Jenny—she could hardly sleep after each letter. All of her excitement about a new and adventurous life in Montana got Duke and Fielding thinking about a farm of their own. Summer months moved on to winter months and due to Jenny's enthusiasm and begging to go west, Ida agreed to go and look after her. Ida was nineteen and reasoned that she might find a cowboy husband in Montana. That persuaded the boys to go to look after both girls.

Jenny could barely control herself while waiting to start the trip down the Ohio River for the May departure from Independence, Missouri. She had always been anxious and curious about what lay around the next bend or over the next hill. For the past three weeks, she had been living her dream, traveling the open road to a distant place full of adventure and surprises. She had not minded the trail- dust riding on the wind, coming from the land of mysteries and intrigue. She had not minded primitive living conditions and the crowded wagon. The hardships encountered were just stepping-stones to a bright and delightful future. She marveled at the birds and insects and wildflowers as she walked and skipped along each new mile. She hungrily inhaled the sweet smell of prairie grass and feasted her astonished eyes on glorious sunsets.

Dear Reader—Here's what Jenny saw almost every evening on the Oregon Trail:

Just before the sun's blushing face would settle below the horizon for the night, the sky was alive with colors of the rainbow in a scope she had never imagined. Angels must have taken great pride in painting their mottled masterpieces. Jenny could visualize angels using giant celestial palettes to mix, and then dab, the colors on Heaven's window, back lighted by the brilliance of God's throne. Soft pinks and violets were blended with a hundred hues of red, as wispy strips of lemon yellow and bursts of gold drifted across the breadth of the serene glory. Gentle, heavenly winds slowly repainted the angel's handiwork into a continuing pageantry of majestic delight. Jenny would forget to breathe as her dreamy eyes were looking at more beauty than at any other time in her life. Her eyes were seeing the sunset, but her heart was throbbing for another joyous tomorrow. There was so much more good than bad that she could have many times flown into the arched sky beyond the vast, treeless prairie.

Last night, when she realized what had happened, the gravity of her sorrow brought her high-flying spirit crashing down. Her many hours of tears turned the dust at her feet into mud. She wished she and Nellie were young again, making mud pies in the warm West Virginia sun. But just before Jerry returned to the cave, she had put her younger days in their place. She then gathered all her hopes and fears and wrapped her most earnest dreams around them.

She knew going on in either direction without Jerry would be unwise—but which way? Her biggest fear was how much to trust him. He had been nice and helpful so far, but what were his true motives? He admitted he was just drifting with the wind, which gave her an opinion about his character and ambition. She had always been around honest, hard-working men. Now, she was compelled to place her life in the trust of a drifting stranger.

"Jenny, we must get movin' quick."

"I don't know you Mist . . . Jerry."

Before she could say anything else, he rather loudly answered her remark. "Listen little Jenny—we have to move now, and guess you will just have to trust me enough to make a decision which way to go."

Her decision was mostly made four hours ago. She just now had the courage to say aloud that her adventurous heart and pioneer spirit had out-voted the practical part of her.

With the finality of a Supreme Court judge, she boldly looked the nervous drifter in the eye. "If you help me get to Montana, I will thank you a thousand times and will always consider you my truest friend. But if you harm me or kill me, I will haunt you till you burn in Hell."

Jerry rolled his eyes and jerked his head back. He suddenly wasn't so sure about being with this little gal for another six weeks.

Chapter 3

They moved on quickly after breakfast...

"Okay Jenny, I'll go back to the wagons and get an ox to carry our food and a cow for milk. If they are true to their nature, they will be grazing near the wagons. While I'm gone, repack the food to have as few boxes as possible."

She had already inventoried the food and knew there would be enough for about three weeks. It was another four weeks to Fort Laramie. She reasoned they would be okay with some wild game and fish and berries. Jerry had done a good job gathering the food from the burned wagons. They had flour, beans, cornmeal, bacon, coffee and tea, honey, dried apples and peaches, sugar and salt and baking soda, and a jar of buttermilk. There was also a sack of hard tack or sea biscuits, and lots of beef jerky. While packing, she was hoping they could find a churn at the wagons to make butter.

Jerry wasn't gone long. While he was strapping the food boxes on the ox, Jenny milked the cow. They drank some and saved the rest to make butter later.

Approaching and stopping at the burned wagons was almost more than Jenny could bear. She saw the graves and wanted to place flowers on each one but knew not to ask for the time. They had walked from the cave with the ox and cow in tow behind the horse.

After a moment of silence, Jerry softy told her, as he pointed, "Ida and Fielding are in these two graves." He told her they were by the wagon where he got the family picture. What he didn't tell her was they both had been scalped and beaten about the face with probably a tomahawk, and he couldn't recognize them from the picture. Jerry started walking toward the wagons to find a churn. He looked back and told Jenny she had three minutes for some flowers and a look through her wagon.

She wanted to stand still and cry but quickly put flowers on the two graves and found another picture of just her Mommy and Poppy. She also found a necklace belonging to Ida. She located her partially burned Oregon Trail Guidebook, journal, and Ida's small shovel she had used for her cooking fires. With tears streaming down her cheeks, Jenny left the black, smelly remains of her West Virginia connection.

In a swift motion, Jerry helped Jenny on the horse and stated with the authority of a wagon train leader as he started walking, "It's late, but we need to make ten miles today. We will eat some dried fruit and jerky after a while and keep moving." He was tired after the grave digging last night but could still walk five miles before his turn to ride.

Jenny needed some easy time to let the past two days ride out of her mind and recapture her enthusiasm to move onward to a new life. She again needed to be excited about the surprises beyond the bends and over the hills. They didn't speak more than a dozen words till stopping for supper.

Jerry had ripped off some wagon boards and Jenny soon had the supper fire ready. The quick fire was accomplished by digging a rectangular hole in the ground about the size of a peck basket. The hole was oriented so the wind would blow through the length of the hole and provide ample oxygen for a hot fire. The menu was fried bacon, skillet cornbread, dried apples boiled in water, and tea with honey.

Two tired pilgrims slept soundly the first night together, on the way to Jenny's new life and what Jerry believed would be just another drifting experience for him.

They moved on quickly after a breakfast of bacon, pancakes with honey, and hot coffee. Both were feeling better after a good night's rest, and Jerry again complimented the cook for another fine meal. She said she was still learning and should keep doing better. There was more conversation, because Jenny asked several questions about flora and fauna she had never seen before. Jerry was glad he could answer most of them satisfactorily.

It was mid-afternoon before Jenny could ask about Duke. Jerry told her he had placed rocks on him, and that he also said a prayer after Duke was well covered. She didn't ask any more, and he didn't say any more. The past hurt was slowly fading, and the faith and trust in Jerry and his consideration for her were rehabilitating her broken spirit.

That night, she got her journal up to date, including all about the sadness, which had suddenly changed her life. Journal entries were always at the end of each day, and the first four were always in the same order; the weather, source and quality of water, availability of wood or buffalo chips for the cooking fire, and quality and quantity of grazing grass for the animals. She would also note any graves or dead oxen or horses beside the trail. While in Independence, Missouri waiting to start, she heard one family, traveling from Illinois to Oregon in the 1850s, counted 226 graves by the Trail.

Jenny went to sleep the second night, believing Jerry was an honorable person and he really would not harm her. She knew her decision to continue west with him was founded on trust, and so far, it appeared she had made the right decision.

The next two days were actually a time of happiness, even with the grief from losing her two brothers and sister. She knew she had to recover quickly and adjust to her new life. She was beginning to laugh a little. She reviewed the trail guidebook purchased in Independence and was getting excited about upcoming landmarks. She was looking forward to seeing Jail Rock, Courthouse Rock, Chimney Rock, Scotts Bluff, and of course, Fort Laramie. Jerry played his fiddle after supper, and Jenny would sing some Stephen Foster songs and several hymns. Her soft voice sweetened the night air around the camp, and if man or beast were passing by, they would surely stop and listen.

At the beginning of the fifth day of their westward trek, something unexpected happened. The day and night before had been a time of laughing and singing. Two strangers had become good friends in just a few days. But on this morning, there was no laughing in the camp.

They awoke at the same time as before, and Jerry attended to the animals. When he returned to camp, Jenny had not started breakfast. She had not even started the morning cook fire. After two attempts, she told Jerry she was cramping and thought she was dying.

He knew the symptoms of cholera and knew victims usually died within twenty-four hours. He looked at her pale face and almost cried. Cramping, vomiting, and diarrhea were the main symptoms he knew about, and he was really scared because he had no medicine to give her. She had not vomited, and he didn't know just how to ask about diarrhea. Before he attempted to ask, she told him that she was surely dying because of the bleeding. Jerry couldn't hold back a smile, as there was no obvious blood to be seen.

He had overheard his mother telling his younger sister about some changes that happen to young girls. Jenny was too busy being a tomboy to ask questions about such things. Her mother and three older sisters didn't volunteer any information. Jerry told her, as tenderly as he could, that the bodies of young girls change when they become young ladies. He told her what was happening was natural and would only last a few days and would repeat, or cycle, every month. He further stated that he didn't know why it happened, but he guessed it was part of God's plan.

Both were too embarrassed to look at each other for hours. They had eaten dried fruit for breakfast, so they had an early lunch, which included coffee. Their embarrassment lessened during the afternoon, and by suppertime, they were laughing again while eating a roasted prairie hen. An unlikely bond was being forged between a dreamer and a drifter that would have to be reckoned with if they were to reach Montana.

Chapter 4

"I won't die on you."

The landmarks and dusty miles were whizzing by, and the weather had been mostly nice for the past two weeks. The only big problem was finding firewood and chips. Since the 1840s, thousands and thousands had traveled the trail and had required tons and tons of fuel for cooking fires. But aside from the fuel shortage, the caravan leaders of a horse named Topsi, an ox named Flori, and a cow named Polly were enjoying comfortable conversation.

The drifter in the person of Jeremiah "Jerry" Bowles was true to his word that his intentions were honorable in helping Jenny get safely to her brother in Montana. He was courteous and kind to his little ward and showed her respect in all ways. The two were now good friends. Jenny trusted him, literally with her life, and in no way did he step over the line of friendship. But within the heart of Jerry's ward, the friendship thing was a little deeper. Riding double with her arms around his waist was causing some unfamiliar vibes in her changing body. It seemed she had matured a month for each day on the trail. After the Indian attack, she had suddenly assumed a woman's responsibility, and her body was quickly catching up with her new role.

The interval between supper and sleep time had been especially meaningful to her the past few nights. Jerry was playing his fiddle and harmonica and she was singing. As a matter of fact, she had been singing a lot during the day for the past fifty miles. The fifteen to twenty hard miles during the day were forgotten when they talked and sang after supper.

The night after passing Chimney Rock was a major turning point in Jenny's young life. The talking sessions before that night had been mostly about her family and her future plans. Jerry had contributed little about his family and his future plans. She knew he was a drifter and didn't pointedly ask why he was aimlessly roaming about.

Earlier that day had been special as to their relationship of boy and girl. Before the noon meal, they washed their faces in clear, cool creek water. It was so refreshing, and for some reason, Jenny felt completely uninhibited with Jerry for the first time since being together. They had cried and laughed and joked together. In the beginning, Jerry was like her surrogate brother, but that was no longer her position. She had never been around a man like him, and had recently concluded fate must have brought them together for some special reason.

They were nearing Fort Laramie, and she wanted her only dress to be clean. So, right in front of Jerry, she removed her blue-checked, gingham dress and washed it in the creek. He didn't seem surprised. They had an unhurried lunch and then headed west.

During the past few weeks, her breasts had suddenly started to enlarge and were more noticeable wearing only her petticoat. If Jerry detected this, he didn't indicate it in any way. Jenny wasn't flaunting her emergence into young womanhood—it just didn't enter her mind. She was comfortable being with Jerry and trusted him to remain the gentleman he had been since fate put them together.

That night after supper, both were quieter than usual. Jenny had her dress back on, and her petticoat had been washed and was drying. The moon was full and brilliant. She had never before looked at a full moon with the same perception as at that moment. Sitting ten feet from Jerry, she sensed an unfamiliar attraction to him as puzzled tears trickled down her warm cheeks. She was feeling a mellowness superimposed on an anxiety that had her inexperienced heart cycling from almost stopping to pounding like a drum. She was sure Jerry could hear and would ask about it. But she was the one who needed to ask a question before her heart did, in fact, burst.

The fire was mostly out—just embers and some sparks that would occasionally flitter upward. Moonlight gleamed on Jerry's suntanned face as he stared at remains of the supper fire. Neither had spoken for minutes. A sudden breeze fanned the hot coals, and a small flame licked the blackened coffeepot as Jenny found the courage to ask her question.

Listen:

"Jerry ... are ... are you married? You have never said anything about ... anything about a wife or even a girlfriend."

So many new things were happening to this little girl from West Virginia. Her face had never been so fiery. Her anxiety had heightened, plus she was feeling ashamed for asking the question. The serenity of the moment before was melting from a strange burning within her five-foot-four shaking body. Her heart was now all pounding, and she unconsciously placed her hands on her chest to keep it from jumping out of her chest. She thought about the cave and their first meal together and how bashful and how afraid she was to be with him. She then remembered how, through the days, they had talked, laughed, sang, and joked about all sorts of silly things. And now, tonight, their companionship was connecting like a circle. She was back to little talking like in the cave, but the fear had changed to something she didn't understand. She wished the question had never been asked. With her head bowed as if praying, Jenny wished the moon would draw her up out of this campsite and cool her burning body. Before another wish or a prayer, Jerry spoke.

"Jenny . . . When I was sixteen, I met a girl one night at a dance. Her name was Jane."

Jenny was now really in trouble—she could hardly breathe. Whatever her feelings and emotions had been before, they were now doubled in magnitude. She thought, "Could this be a sign?" Her name was Jane, but she had always been called Jenny. Jerry continued just before Jenny felt like she would faint.

"She died two days before our wedding day." His words were forced—words from a chapter in his life that he was trying to forget.

Jenny couldn't decide if she was sad for him or glad for herself. Before her spinning head had a chance to decipher her true feelings, he pushed out more strained words.

"I left Marietta and started driftin'. For weeks and months all I did was draw pictures of her. I even drew a picture of the two of us standing in front of our dream house we designed together."

He lowered his head, but Jenny could see a grimace on his face from confessing why he became a drifter. She, too, had lately become a drifter. She had been drifting on waves of joy and on winds of delight that were blowing her changing body off course. Jerry looked at her flushed face as he spoke with sincerity.

"I've been holdin' back from loving someone else—afraid she would also die."

When Jenny heard the word "love," her body actually twitched, and she was not breathing again.

She quickly realized what was happening to her. She had never completely connected their friendly relationship with love. It was a word she had considered in a different context. Without consulting her mind, her heart prompted her next words spoken in a muffled voice. "I won't die on you."

"What! What did you say?"

"Uh . . . uh, I said were you sad and blue?"

Jerry looked at her in disbelief. He thought he made it

clear about his sadness and melancholy. He had been forced to remember Jane again after Jenny's friendship was beginning to bridge an emptiness he once believed was a permanent chasm in his life. He slowly stood and walked out on the prairie. The moon was so bright that Jenny could see each time he kicked something as he walked around and around the camp. She was on her bedroll when he returned from his walk. She closed her eyes and tried to assess whatever state of happiness or state of confusion that possessed her.

She had moved to a different level tonight but couldn't decide if it was higher or lower. There was so much indecisiveness churning within her that she began to cry. The tears burned both her eyes and heart, while her mind demanded answers. "Why is this happening to me? I lost two brothers and a sister and now I'm losing Jerry." She couldn't find an answer to the dilemma before sleep stilled her confusion.

The next morning was bright and calm. They were only eight to ten miles from Fort Laramie, and both were excited about a change in their routine. Jenny briefly looked back over the last few days and earnestly believed it was the happiest time she would ever have in her life. So many happy changes were linked together before last night, she guessed they could be chained around her heart and bind sweet memories there forever.

When she and Jerry met, she knew she was a child. But now, she was a responsible team member like her nineteen-year-old sister, Ida, had been. She was cooking, milking the cow, and doing everything else at the campsites. Jerry took care of the animals, gathered wood and chips, and provided wild game and fish. Many times she even helped some with fuel and wild game and fish. Jenny Supples knew what she could do physically and knew she was useful. But she couldn't stop the fluttering in her heart, and she couldn't make Jerry see her as a mature person—or at least a *maturing* person.

There was no reference to last night as they ate breakfast, hurriedly broke camp, and got on the trail. Conversation during the morning hours was mostly what Jerry knew about the fort. Jenny contributed some information from her Oregon Trail Guidebook.

During the afternoon, the two weary travelers gradually reverted to their happy, carefree ways as they laughed and joked along the hot dusty miles. That was before riding double. Jerry was again quiet. Jenny was also silent and contented to be close to a man she was afraid to trust or touch a month ago.

When she put her arm around his waist, conflicting feelings returned—mostly sad ones. She was beginning to believe in her heart she was still a mere child in his eyes, and he would be moving on after Montana. But for these few, precious moments, she was making a memory that could be recalled long after he was gone.

Chapter 5

. . . a delightful feeling surrounded Jenny.

Seven and a half weeks after leaving Independence, Missouri, Jerry and Jenny, riding double on Topsi, led Flori and Polly through shallow water as they crossed the Laramie River. Fort Laramie was situated in the southeastern part of the Wyoming Territory. The fort, on high ground overlooking the river, was a welcome sight. It was built in 1834 as a trading post and was still a major trail stopover in 1883.

While the animals were splashing through the water, Jenny wanted to squeeze Jerry a little tighter and lay her head on his back. She was so proud of him. At that moment, it was admiration—not love. He had kept his promise about helping on the journey and not harming her. For that, she was truly thankful.

The cottonwood tree leaves were really dancing in a warm, late afternoon breeze, which made her remember some other breezes back down the trail that had become violent thunderstorms. She had heard about prairie storms but was not prepared for the two they had survived. The lightning was nothing short of spectacular, but she had been too scared to watch all the time. She couldn't believe the amount of rain that soaked them in a forty-five minute deluge. Hail the size of her fist was boldly recorded in her journal.

Fort Laramie, with its brownish-yellow colored adobe bricks, was indeed a welcome view. It was a place to rest and a place to hear news about the trail ahead, including any known hostile Indians. Letters could be written and posted. Women could get a good meal they didn't have to cook. The fort had storerooms containing trail-related items for sale or trade. Jerry had gotten extra salt from the burned wagons, which he used to trade for new clothing. All of the remaining dried beans were traded for beef jerky. Jenny had quickly discovered too much fuel was required to cook beans. The fort was also a place where fur traders and mountain men could celebrate after a long, cold, and lonely winter.

The Indian massacre news had preceded them. It was witnessed from a distance by a man, who told another man, who was presently at the fort. Everyone was anxious to hear details. Several men gathered in a trading room and heard what really happened when the six wagons were attacked and burned. They learned Jenny had lost two brothers and a sister. Jerry claimed she was about the same as an orphan after the attack, so he was taking her to Montana to live with another brother.

Just before dark, Jerry heard a scream and then heard a man say he could use a pretty orphan to keep him warm on cold, winter nights. When Jerry got to Jenny, the smelly mountain man had a dirty hand over her mouth. He was half-carrying and half-dragging her to his tent. Jerry ran and jumped on his back, causing him to let go of Jenny.

The fight that followed was talked about long after the fighters recovered and went their separate ways.

Jerry was not as big as the filthy beast, but he was strong and madder than he had ever been. No one was going to harm *his* Jenny.

After Jerry jumped on the beast's back, they both hit the ground. Jerry took a hard punch on the back of his neck as they scrambled to their feet. Then Jerry jabbed a powerful left that flattened the mountain man's nose and knocked him backward. The hairy creature almost lost his footing but lunged forward. Jerry stopped his advance with a hard right near his left ear. This time the smelly hunk of garbage went to his knees. When he got up, he was swinging a knife. The first swing missed as Jerry sidestepped and lost his balance and then fell to the ground.

This next part has been told at least two different ways.

With Jerry on the ground, the burly mountain man dived on him with his knife ready to do business. Jerry managed to roll enough so the knife missed his heart and bounced off a rib, making an ugly cut as revealed through his slashed shirt. He continued to roll, quickly jumped to his feet, and drove his boot to the back of the beast's head, pushing his face to the ground. Jenny's protector then pounced on a broad back, directing his knees to land on the kidnapper's kidneys, and then started giving him rights and lefts to the sides of his head.

The mountain man didn't survive winters just holed up in a cave. He had fought man and beast often and could take a heap of punishment before being counted out. With reserve strength, he flipped Jerry off his back. The two side-stepped in a circle for two rounds—some said three. The man with the knife was eager to bring more blood Jerry didn't need to lose as his tan shirt was already turning red. After either two or three circles, the biggest French trapper Jerry had ever seen, found stomach flesh with his big knife. Some said Jerry took the knife to get close enough to land more punches–and punch he did. He had also found some reserve energy, but blood loss was fast draining the ration. Regardless, he was thinking about that filthy varmint holding Jenny and was still beating after the trapper was unconscious. Three men were required to pull Jerry off and stop his swinging.

Jenny ran to the side of the one who had just saved her life, again. A man stopped the bleeding and said the ten-inch long stomach cut was bad and would take a long time to heal. Jenny cradled his head in her lap and cooled his face with a wet cloth someone put in her hand.

Jenny's family attended a small Baptist Church near Winfield, West Virginia. At a Sunday night service when she was eleven, she accepted Jesus as her personal Savior. She believed Jesus died for her sins and she trusted Him to help her get through this earthly life, so she could then spend eternity in Heaven. She knew the Bible was God's Holy, Inspired Word and knew prayer was a way to talk with God. When rattlesnakes attacked Duke, she prayed he would not die. But God's answer was not what she expected. After the snake incident, after she learned about her other brother and sister, and when she realized she was alone with a stranger, she prayed for the Lord to keep her safe.

> *Dear Lord, you know I'm young and can be a witness for you and glorify your name for many years to come. Please keep me safe and don't let me die now like my brothers and sister. Amen.*

Jenny didn't realize it during the first few hours in the cave, but God answered her prayer in the person of Jeremiah Bowles. God put Jerry by her side at the right time, and her life was spared.

Now, almost two months later, God's answer to her prayer was resting in her lap and might be dying because he risked his life to keep her safe. Tears from a little girl, who sprang into a young woman almost over night, were falling on the most beautiful face she had ever seen. Regardless of her prior confusion about the strange and wonderful feelings, she knew, at this instant, the meaning of love. With all her heart and soul she loved Jerry. She prayed for the Lord to let him live. Right now, during these precious moments while cradling his head in her lap, she wasn't thinking about her life—just Jerry's. He had won the fight to save her but could be losing the battle for his chance to live and enjoy making music and all the other things he liked to do.

Jerry was moved to a cot in the fort. An old Indian woman, who was a cook at the fort, took over caring for him. She doctored him with certain herbs, roots, and tree bark; and he gained strength during the first week after the fight. Then, in the middle of the second week, he lapsed into unconsciousness. The stomach wound was seriously infected. Jenny had been by his side every possible minute and was encouraged with his improvement. But as she now looked at his pale face, she anguished with each of his shallow breaths.

In a dimly lit room, just past midnight, Jenny prayed aloud as she gently clasped his hand between her hands.

> *Dear Lord, I'm the little girl you gave an adventurous heart that caused me to start on this trip. You have made me healthy and strong. I have survived a lot of hardships and have accepted losing my brothers and sister as your will. But dear Lord, please don't take Jerry. I know that he will probably leave me after we get to Billings, but please let him live. He risked his life to save mine. Please, dear Lord, take that in account. He deserves to live. This is what I think. Amen.*

After the prayer, a delightful feeling surrounded Jenny. It was like a warm blanket around her on a cold night, and she was soon asleep. Right at sunrise, Jerry awoke her when he asked, "Hey Miss Jenny, could a fellow get a cup of coffee in this place?"

She jumped to full awareness and saw his familiar smile revealing his beautiful, white teeth. She started crying and kissed his cheek. After the prayer, the infectious wound had erupted, and enough poison drained to allow his survival spirit to take charge.

Jenny enjoyed the time at the fort while Jerry was getting progressively stronger. She wrote several letters to family and friends in West Virginia and particularly enjoyed prepared meals. She and Jerry became friends with a family from Kentucky who were heading to California. They were looking for a new start in the fertile valleys of the thirty-first state of the Union.

The traveling to Fort Laramie had been only a few slow miles each day, but Jenny's mind had been on a fast track. She had new responsibilities after the Indian attack, and there was always the fear of another attack. She and Jerry were becoming closer than they realized, and her thoughts were mostly disconnected without any clear conclusions. Since the fight, she had been too worried about Jerry to think about much of anything else until she knew he would recover.

During a relaxing warm afternoon in a moment of delight, she remembered some of the beautiful flowers along the trail: yellow, white, and lavender Foxglove; blue and purple Larkspur; pink Rose Moss; and large, yellow blooms of Prickly Pear. She also had time for some deep thinking. She had time to put her life in perspective with her present situation and to assess the forces within and around her.

She was well aware of the age difference between Jerry and herself but couldn't envision her uncertain future without him. Many perplexing thoughts tumbled in and out of her relaxed, but still confused, mind.

Before she left West Virginia, and before the Indian attack, her future was jubilantly planned. She would slowly and enjoyably mature in Billings and then marry and live happily ever after. But around a bend in her planned dreams, a handsome prince appeared one day and saved her from certain death. Now her fairy tale life was no longer planned the way she dreamed.

They spent another two weeks at the fort after Jerry recovered from his setback, and then they changed their direction from west to north.

Chapter 6

. . . a different kind of closeness . . .

Billings was located by the Yellowstone River in south-central Montana Territory and was no more than another month from Fort Laramie. From her trail guide, Jenny learned that the areas of the Wyoming and Montana Territories, west of the Rocky Mountain range, were actually part of the large Oregon Territory.

The first day on the trail to Billings was a relearning experience. Relatively luxurious living at the fort was missed as they resumed cooking over an open fire and sleeping on the ground in the wild Wyoming country. Jenny did most of the work, and she walked while Jerry rode the horse. She gathered all the wood and chips, milked the cow, made butter, and cooked. It wasn't much different from before, except for gathering fuel—Jerry couldn't safely bend over much.

After the first week on their new course, they were again seasoned pioneers. Jenny was still maturing at double speed and believed she looked and acted at least sixteen. The daytime and evening routines were comfortable, and they were embracing all the wonders and beauties of God's world in a more intense manner. They were both truly appreciative and thankful they were still alive.

The experiences at the fort were another major turning point in Jenny's young life, and she believed Jerry might have reassessed his purpose in life. They hadn't talked directly about what happened, but she felt a different kind of closeness to Jerry and sensed he might be viewing her differently than before. Yes, she knew something more endearing had happened between them but wouldn't let her heart stray too far from the bare truth of their nine year age difference.

Most of their conversation was merry and even silly. Jerry was a prankster and had even scared her to tears—albeit, happy tears. She had retaliated to the best of her ability, and the result was a lot of fun on a lonely trail.

As Jerry Bowles escorted a young girl to Montana, he protected her from wild animals and wild mountain men and made her laugh. But there wasn't much laughter the day they crossed the Yellowstone River near the mouth of Clark's Fork. Riding double, they made ten miles down the river trail before two tense travelers camped together for the last time. Ten more miles the next day would have them in Billings by mid-afternoon.

Before they found a campsite, Jenny was starting to feel the dreadful pangs of loneliness. She knew Jerry was going to leave her. She had tried to persuade her jumbled mind and heart that he would stay because he loved her. But for the past two days, even with all the joking and laughing, she could feel in her bones that he would be leaving.

With a forlorn ache in her tense body, she asked Jerry a question. "Do you miss the States?"

She really meant she was beginning to miss the security and order of her home state east of the Mississippi River. They had traveled through the relatively new states of Kansas and Nebraska, the Territory of Wyoming, and had just entered Montana Territory. She would soon be with a brother she hadn't seen since she was five years old, and without Jerry, the excitement and glamour of the West had turned into dread. Jerry didn't answer. She thought, "Oh, if Ida could only be with me." She was so overcome with a dejected feeling that she didn't even try to guess what he was thinking.

The camp that night was quiet. Jerry pretended to fish while Jenny cooked their last evening meal. She wiped tears as a flood of memories paraded through her melancholy mind. Jerry managed some half smiles during the meal, and as always, praised her cooking. "You're a good cook, Jenny."

She smiled and looked into his cheerless, blue eyes for a second or two before turning away. Cleanup was slow. She took extra time packing—for the last time. Normally they would be singing and laughing after supper, but now Jerry was back down by the river. Jenny walked down and stood close behind him and didn't lose any more time before asking what was burning inside her. "You're going to leave after delivering me to my brother?"

There was no answer.

In a more pleading tone than she intended, "Jerry! Could you please tell me why? I told you in the beginning that if you didn't harm me or kill me I would thank you and—"

Jerry immediately interrupted and answered her louder than he had ever before. "And did I harm you?"

Jenny knew he was also tense, and in an effort to ease the strained conversation, she softy replied, "Oh Jerry, you didn't, and I thank you a thousand times over. You almost died because of me, and . . . I . . . I . . . Oh Jerry, only a true friend would risk their life for someone."

Jenny had promised herself she wouldn't cry where he could see. She had concealed her true feelings for much too long. She spun around and hugged the man who had saved her life.

A few uncontrollable tears, mingled with the intent of her heart, produced some soggy words that expressed her most sincere thankfulness. "Oh Jerry, I thank you and thank you. I only wish you knew how much I . . . how much . . . I . . . I thank you."

It was only a brief embrace. It seemed they both knew to back away. Jenny had wanted to say, "I wish you knew how much I love you."

Before she could reconnect her heart with her mind, Jerry reluctantly mumbled barely distinguishable words. "I have to move on. There's something I have to do."

The moment of truth she had been dreading was still ringing in her ears when she asked, "Can't you tell me what it is?"

"It's . . . it's . . . No, it's something with my family. That's all I can say now. I don't know how long it will take."

"Jerry, we have been through so much together. Can't you tell me why you have to leave me—don't I mean more to you than just a girl needin' help on the trail?"

Jenny's face was suddenly blood red and burning. She had wanted to ask that sooner, but now she was embarrassed for saying it.

"Jenny, Jenny, I want to stay with you, but I ran away from this responsibility before I met you. It's a family matter, and I have to go."

The way he said, "I have to go" sounded like he would, indeed, go. She was disappointed and maybe a little angry, but not out of control of her wits as she kindly asked, "Would you allow me to ask one more favor before you leave?"

"Yes! Anything."

"Could you stay with me a couple of days after we find my brother?"

"Yes, yes, as long as you need me."

She wanted to say "for the rest of my life," but she didn't, and she didn't sleep well for thinking about that "something" he had to do.

On September 7th, Brother Charles greeted her with love and affection, declaring how she had grown and how much she looked like Mamma. He then changed to the role of a big brother.

"I expected you a month ago. Where's Duke and Fielding and Ida?"

Jenny looked up at her big brother, who was about the size of the mountain man at the fort. He also had a black beard, but it was neatly trimmed. He had a barrel chest, broad shoulders, and muscular arms, which looked like they could squeeze a bear to death.

Charles was waiting for an answer as he glanced at Jerry who was outside the butcher shop. "Who is that man, and where are the others?"

"Brother Charles, they didn't make it."

"What do you mean? Poppy said in his letter that they left with you."

"We all left together, but Indians and rattlesnakes got them three weeks out of Independence."

Charles looked out at Jerry and then to Jenny. He focused back on Jerry.

"Brother Charles, his name is Jerry Bowles and he helped me get here."

Still staring through the window at Jerry, Charles' deep voice boomed, "Did this man harm you?"

"No! No! He saved my life."

Both Jerry and Jenny saw Charles' clinched fists relax as he looked back to Jenny. "Then you are all right? You look healthy."

"Yes, yes, I'm fine. It's been a long trip."

"Come child, and tell me all about what happened. Tell the man to come in. What's his name?"

Jerry left three days later. Charles liked him, and they quickly became friends. Jerry the prankster and Charles the circus clown made for lots of laughs. The ex-clown was always blurting silly "one liners." Jenny never forgot two of them:

"After my milkin', goin' to do some quiltin'.
Break it and shake it and hang it on the wall,
and don't let it fall."

But there was no silly talk or pranks the night before Jerry left. Charles told several circus stories to a couple who didn't really hear them. Before they retired, Jenny thanked Jerry one more time but didn't ask again that he stay. He wished her good luck with her new home; those were his last words. She knew he would be gone before another sunrise.

Before dawn, he headed south to Fort Laramie. He would then go back to Independence, Missouri. Jerry Bowles left behind a rapidly maturing young girl who loved him so much she cried every night for a month after he left. She was in a place she didn't like and with a brother she didn't know. She also missed Duke and Fielding and her sister Ida.

Jerry left something behind that caused most of her tears. A bundle of sketches were in the kitchen the next morning. She knew he sketched often, and several were of her. Most of his drawings were pencil sketches of landmarks, which he showed her as they were finished. What she didn't know was he had later drawn her in front of various landmarks and prairie scenes. She could hardly believe her eyes when she first viewed them. He also left five twenty-dollar gold coins and fifteen silver dollars. (This was probably the amount found in Fielding's pockets.)

After six weeks, she started expecting a letter from Jerry. By that time, she had made some friends but was still home-sick and still missed him. The sketches were reviewed often, but by November, she was beginning to feel he would never return to her. She was then working full time in the general store and knew everyone for miles around. The little pioneer girl wouldn't be fourteen for another five months but already looked and acted much older. The relatively busy days in the store weren't too bad, but long, cold nights were depressing and lonely.

One cold afternoon in mid-November, Jenny was talking to Naomi Bolts about the weather. Naomi was a widow and said she and her late husband would discuss the weather often in connection with their crops. She then reminisced a little about the good times she and her husband had together. Jenny asked how she was coping without him. Naomi smiled and said they had forty-seven good years together, and she accepted God's plan in their life. She talked about loneliness and responsibilities since her husband passed. Naomi then told Jenny that to be with him again in Heaven was what kept her going onward each day.

With a glint of sadness in her eyes, Jenny volunteered, "I once knew a person for a little over forty-seven days, and I miss him every day and night." She hesitated before continuing, "It's not now as painful as when I first got here."

"Oh my dear child—you are so young to be missin' somebody. Is he . . . did he . . . did he pass away?"

"Maybe. I haven't heard from him for months. I—"

Naomi interrupted. "Well honey, was he a family member? You are so young to—"

"No family member—a man who saved my life and helped me get to Billings. Yes, I know I'm young but old enough to be in love. Or maybe I should say 'used to be in love,' because I'm beginning to realize that our short time together is all the Lord is going to permit."

Each cold Montana day and night seemed to be a week long till Jenny finally turned the calendar to December. A few warmer days in early December lifted her spirits enough to at least think a little about Christmas. Warmer days didn't last long before a cold wind arrived with more snow than Jenny had ever seen. She and Charles lived in back of the store, so the heavy snow didn't restrict her working.

There were no customers that morning, but later in the day, she was rather busy. While she was waiting on a customer, Charles entered the store and casually said, "Here's a letter for you." He put it on the counter and went to the butcher shop.

Jenny waited on two other customers and forgot about the letter. She had been receiving letters often from West Virginia family members and friends, and she assumed this letter was from home.

Charles later re-entered the store and asked, "Ain't you goin' to read your letter? Who do you know in Independence?"

"No one I can think of."

Jenny Supples had had some happy joyous moments in her young life. But when she opened the letter, all her other happiness was secondary to the exalted feeling at that moment.

> *Dear Jenny*
> *I made it back to Independence OK. When*
> *I stopped at Fort Laramie the mountain man*
> *was there but he left quick. I will be movin' on*
> *soon. I think of you often.*
> *Jerry*

Jenny had a radiant glow on her face. It may have even brightened the room. She would have been the happiest girl in the world had he written that he was coming back to Billings. But the part about thinking of her often would keep her rapturous for a long, long time. She was still perplexed, however, about the secrecy of the "something" he had to do. And also, if he ever intended to return, why didn't he ask her to wait until he fulfilled his family obligation?

When Jerry was in Independence the April before, he received a letter from his mother. His younger sister, Evelina, was not getting any better, and his mother proposed he take her to some western state where the air was drier. Evelina was his favorite sister. She had consumption (tuberculosis). He wanted to help, but at that time he was still hurting and missing his lost love, Jane. Actually, he was angry his life should be turned up side down again so soon after losing her. That's when he started westward. He knew he was drifting from a responsibility but could only think of one day at a time. Several times he vowed to return to Independence and wait for Evelina to arrive.

Just after the noon meal of the second day with the wagon train, he had decided to spend one more night and then leave to help his sister. But the hands of fate had a more pressing problem for Jeremiah Bowles. He was confronted with Jenny Supples.

The weeks rolled by, and the more he thought about taking care of Jenny, a stranger, the more he felt obligated to help his sister. At the same time, he was falling in love with Jenny, but their age difference kept his true feelings churning inside his compassionate heart. Many times he wanted to tell Jenny about Evelina but believed he alone had to decide what to do.

After a few weeks, Evelina arrived in Independence. They took the Santa Fe Trail to New Mexico to begin her recovery. He had decided to care for her and couldn't make any permanent plans with Jenny. He didn't feel it fair to tell Jenny he might return to her, when his responsibility to his sister was first priority for as long as she needed him. If he had discussed this with Jenny, she would have gladly gone to New Mexico to be with the man she loved. Some decisions in life are made more from obligations than from feelings of the heart. Jerry thought a great deal about Jenny and was sorry he didn't include her in his plan to care for his sister. His life wasn't turning out like he once dreamed. Jenny had been a second chance for happiness, but he walked away from her.

Chapter 7

"... a good day for a buggy ride..."

Jenny somehow survived her first Montana winter. She didn't think spring would ever arrive or that she would ever be warm again. Her heart almost stopped with each letter she received that long lonely winter, but no more came from Jerry. Summer was hotter than she thought possible, and she could hardly believe she was looking forward to winter. The butcher shop and general store were busy. Jenny was so well liked that Charles often remarked people came in just to see his beautiful sister. He was sure that was true with one young boy around sixteen or seventeen. Jenny was fourteen and fully matured in manner and form. She and the young boy had been to two socials, and all the boys and men wanted to dance with her.

Jerry could never be fully forgotten, but it was getting easier to accept the fact that if he really cared, he would have returned by now. She wasn't thinking about marrying "that boy" or anyone soon. She was, however, beginning to like Montana and believed she would someday marry a local man and settle down to raise a family.

The sixth of July 1884, was an interesting day for Jenny. Before she got out of bed, a glow or a flush or something warm filled her entire body. She thought it was a fever, but she didn't feel sick. Jubilation flooded her senses all through the day. It was like a burden had been lifted. And with the celebration in her heart, Jerry was foremost in her mind. She would never completely forget him, but she was beginning to turn a page in her life and get excited again about the next bend in the road. She would always pray for Jerry's safety and happiness.

The day ended with nothing special happening. That night, she didn't sleep well and dreamed about the fight at the fort. Only this time, the mountain man won. The next day, Jenny was depressed—just the opposite from her delightful yesterday. She couldn't decide what was on her mind and what would cheer her. After a dismal morning, she decided to look at Jerry's sketches again. The afternoon customers at the general store laughed with the Jenny they loved.

The remaining days of July and August were hot and dusty. Days slipped into weeks, and on the first Thursday in September, John Clarke asked Jenny to marry him. His father owned the feed store, and someday the store would be his. He was eighteen and a nice and kind young man. Jenny was thinking about it.

The next Thursday in September began crisp but not too cold. By noon, it was a pleasant day and would have been a good day for a buggy ride, had it not been a workday. Just before noon, John stopped at the store to take Jenny to lunch. He often came early, and if no one was in the store, he would bend over the counter and kiss the most beautiful girl in Montana and the whole world.

On this beautiful day, luck was with John, and he kissed her two times. Jenny didn't resist. She was close to accepting his proposal even though, at times, she would feel Jerry near.

A little while later, they were seated in the dining room at the Hotel. Bea the waitress remarked, "Well! Jenny isn't you popular today? Another handsome man was just askin' about you."

"What do you mean, Bea?"

"What do I mean? Just what I said—another handsome man was askin' about you."

Not too much concerned, Jenny asked what he looked like as she smiled at John.

"Well, he had black, wavy hair and the purtiest white teeth I ever seen."

Jenny was still looking at the one who had asked to marry her when Bea started her description of the stranger. By the time "white teeth" was spoken, Jenny was standing and screamed, "When was this, and where is he now?"

"Well now, let me think, I waited on Luke and then—"

Jenny screamed again, "Bea! Tell me—How long ago did you see him?"

"Well, I'm tryin' to—maybe twenty or thirty minutes."

Jenny was crying as she pleaded, "Oh Bea, where did he go?"

Bea pointed. "Out that door."

Bea saw the forlorn look on John's face that changed to a pain-racked frown as he watched Jenny run out the door.

Jenny asked everyone if they had seen a black-haired stranger in the past few minutes. Some would ask what he was wearing or would want to talk to her. But she hurried on to someone else as she ran down one side of the street while calling to the other side. No one had seen a stranger until she got to the barbershop where the street forked left and right. Oakie was sitting on the small front porch.

"Yeah Jenny. I seen that man that brung you here last year."

She was about out of breath when she further asked, "How long Oakie—How long ago?"

She grasped a post for support and thought for sure she was going to faint. To think she could have missed the rest of life with Jerry by twenty minutes . . . but that was not going to happen to the little gal from West Virginia. She was gulping much needed air as burning tears streamed down her face.

"Not long Jenny, maybe ten, fifteen—"

Jenny didn't let him finish. "Which way?"

As he pointed, Jenny turned and may have broken a sprint record getting to the livery stable. She rented a rig and dusted

Oakie as she made the turn down the road to her happiness. She was pressing the horse to find the only man she would ever really love.

A lone eagle was riding a warm air current and saw a cloud of dust made by a buckboard wagon speeding down the road and closing in fast on a horse and a rider. The road was hilly, and the buckboard driver couldn't see the horse and rider but the eagle could. The horse's head was drooped, and the rider was slumped in the saddle.

Jerry had made a seven-week trip in just four weeks. He was tired and didn't care what happened to him next. He remembered he mentioned "God's will" one time to Jenny. Right now, he was not too happy with what was just "willed" to him when he looked through the store window.

The horse and despondent rider slowly moved over the crest of a hill. Jenny still couldn't see Jerry and was beginning to think Oakie was mistaken and it wasn't him at all or . . . Oh, she didn't know what to think. She had, so many times, anxiously awaited the surprise around the next bend or over the next hill. But right now, as she neared the top of this hill, there was no anxiety constricting her breathing, or any great expectation of a wondrous surprise awaiting her. For some unexplained reason, she was giving up. If Oakie had seen Jerry, she should have overtaken him by now. She believed it must have been mistaken identity. Suddenly, all of her excitement and determination were soaked with burning tears. She had just lost the man she loved.

Then! As Jenny topped the hill—the eagle saw it all. She raced to Jerry's side and pulled him off the horse. In a happy embrace, they danced around and around, making about as much dust as she had stirred up with the buckboard. The eagle made an extra circle watching two hearts rejoice but couldn't hear what they were saying.

Let's listen:

". . . don't you ever leave me again."

"I won't. I wouldn't have left this time, except I thought I was too late when I saw you kissing in the store."

Jenny was crying too hard to respond.

The eagle left before two happy pioneers stopped kissing and calmed enough for Jerry to explain about his mysterious mission.

Jerry was having trouble talking. Jenny's face was shrouded in some kind of radiant sparkle reflecting a brilliance that was distracting him. But he continued, "Evelina was getting better and had met a man. But then on July the sixth, she just died."

"Oh Jerry."

Jenny then looked away and remembered it was an early July day when she had felt so good. She couldn't sort out her feelings just then. Jerry continued before she had a chance to try.

"They, her friends, were on a hayride and a sudden rain soaked them all. Evelina's consumption got worse and she didn't recover."

Jerry tied his horse to the buggy and took the reins. Jenny was quickly close beside him on the seat. Before they started back to town, she looked at the man who saved her life and whom she dearly loved. The little girl from West Virginia declared in a most positive tone, "I'm going to marry you Mister"

"That's a good idea Missy."

"When I was young, that's what happened, my sweet grand-children. That's why I settled in Montana."

Grandmother Jenny lowered her head and sighed. "All of my West Virginia family is gone. You know Nellie went just last month. I'm the last one. I miss your grandfather, Jerry, but I'm sure he's happy in Heaven. It's so lonely without him. I had many special moments in my life after meeting your grandfather. I'm sure the day I found him, when he was leaving town, would be the most special. But then, I can't forget the first time I cooked for him in the cave. I was scared and afraid I was going to die. But when he complimented me on my slam-johns, well, that was special to a little thirteen year old girl."

Jenny smiled as if remembering each day of her life, and then in mellow, lyrical words she continued, "Ah children, there's so many memories. I relive some everyday. Remember when I said to your grandfather, 'I won't die on you,' and I didn't."

"Granny, you're the best storyteller ever."

"Now Mary, you and Rachel go to sleep. Your Granny is getting tired."

Rachel's big brown eyes were shining when she said, "Maybe someday I can be a good storyteller like you Granny."

The End

About the Author

Harry Beckett is a retired Engineer living in Barboursville, WV with his wife, Betty. Harry dreamed of writing a novel during his career of technical writing and his dream came true in 2002 when his first book was published. This book is his second with more planned during his retirement.

www.ingramcontent.com/pod-product-compliance
Lightning Source LLC
Chambersburg PA
CBHW030544200626
46812CB00020BA/1802